AF424991

First Printing, 2020

ISBN 9798676041144

AmbroseHorneWriting@gmail.com

*To my lottery-prize of a Family, without whom I wouldn't be here in
so many more ways than one*

Jane's Color

Everyone knows the Wallowfords. And I do really mean everyone.

Harold and Maggie Wallowford appeared one day at Fairburn University of Art, the most backwater art school in the most backwater town imaginable. They proceeded to take their small pond by storm. Their final projects for entry-level classes were sent to art shows in Paris. Pieces that were assigned as a weekend homework diversion were selling at auction for sums with more than ten digits. Within moments they were fabulously rich. By the time they graduated the couple were universally declared the definitive artists of the decade, and throughout the next they continued to put out only the most thoughtfully crafted works.

After some time, however, they grew bored of the artistry world, and stopped producing.

For a long five years, referred to only as the Dark Times, the Wallowford Estate remained silent. Nothing was seen or heard of either of them, or any of their household.

After 1,831 days, on the morning of the ninth of April, they broke the silence with a stunning landscape of FUA at sunset, large enough that the police received multiple panicked reports that morning claiming that the sun rose in the west. Flyers covered the ground around it. They advertised an online application for a year-long stay at the Wallowford Estate, wherein the three would create something of an artist's colony.

As expected, applications boomed, both for the program and the college. April 9th became a local holiday in Fairburn. The Board of Regents changed their logo to the famed landscape, sparking a billion-dollar trend for most major corporations of the world to commission the couple to redesign their logo. Fairburn University of Art became known as the Princeton of Visual Arts, and Fairburn its New York. Gaining a Wallowford Program acceptance became something akin to becoming Poet Laureate.

And, as it soon became obvious, a free ticket to luxury. Every single person who was accepted to the Wallowford Program without exception became a recluse. Projects done within that program sold for hundreds of millions of dollars, and all the alumni sold at least five pieces before the year was out. They would move off to some undisclosed location to liberate their work, become recluses like their mentors. And every once and awhile, one of them would release a new piece, each selling for more and more and more.

Yes, everyone knew the Wallowfords and their pupils. But not everyone knew Jane. Until, that is, she was accepted.

There weren't a few reporters at the Wallowford front gates that morning. There was a horde.

A path had been cleared from the road to the gates like a red carpet, and just like at a red carpet, photographers, journalists, and fans crowded each side for a glimpse of the lucky icon-to-be. Peering from the window of her paid-for taxi, Jane couldn't help but feel just a touch overwhelmed at seeing the hundred-odd people arrayed miles from Fairburn, all for her. It was all a far cry from drawing comics at midnight by her nightlight because her roommate was asleep.

Besides, there was the issue of her family.

The taxi driver got out and opened the door for her, then went to pull her suitcase out of the trunk.

"Thanks." She offered, letting the driver lead the way to the gates, hopefully the ones to some sort of freedom.

"Of course." The driver smiled.

She had told her mom, of course. There were practical things, like moving out of a dorm, that had to be done. As for the others, she knew her mom wasn't in touch with her dad or little brother, but she hadn't contacted them for years either. And now the gates, and after that, possibly, a manor all to her own. It was likely that she could go her whole life without seeing them again.

All along the short twenty-five odd feet from the car door to the gates, people launched their questions for the new protege. What was she expecting out of her year there? Had she said goodbye to her parents? What inspired her work? How might her work change? And things of the like. To Jane it just felt like everyone decided to yell at her all at once.

There were some less interrogative bystanders, like a highschool girl in a long coat that said Jane was her role model. Jane wasn't sure if that scared her more or less than the reporters.

And then, of course, the clock struck noon.

From some unfindable source Jane heard loud, booming chimes, like what she would imagine the medieval Parisian heard when Notre Dame's clocktower went off. The crowd fell silent, then unified in noise again as someone began to count aloud and the collective lizard-brain of the populace decided it needed to join in.

At Twelve the mob cheered, for an older couple emerged from the front door and walked down the driveway to meet her. Jane smiled. They looked like they belonged in a fifties sitcom, in a cute and endearing way. Their cardigans were complementary, she noticed. His a dark, burnt orange, and hers a lighter blue-green.

They walked silently, arm in arm. It didn't feel quite right, having two confirmed artistic deities physically present in our mundane world, however separated by the gate and fence. Even they felt mildly uncomfortable out of the Manor, or at least it seemed so to Jane.

A trio of what looked more like washed-up former FUA linemen than proper bouncers pushed their way to the front of the crowd, backing everyone away from the gate. One gestured to Jane, a universal "C'mon, let's get you through here". Jane obliged to the further cheers of the crowd, reaching an auditory climax as she approached that all-important border. Only a yard or so in front of her, without any wrought iron between them, stood the Wallowfords themselves.

With a deep breath, Jane's feet touched the grounds outside Wallowford Manor for the last time.

A final cheer rang out through the crowd, dying into the buzzing sounds of individual conversation as groups of people formed within the mob and decided what they would do, whether retire home or to a meal or watch the Protege make the procession into Wallowford Manor proper.

Jane couldn't hear these, of course. She got caught in the process of introduction with the artistically divine.

"Hello, Mr. and Mrs. Wallowford." Jane began something of a prepared opener. "Thank you so much for…"

"Oh hush," Mrs. Wallowford patted Jane's arm with her free one. "Please, you're going to be with us all year. I'm Maggie, and he's Harold." She looked up at her husband. "Speaking of you, Harold, are you going to grab her bags?"

Harold smiled, disentangling his arm and walking to the bags. "Of course."

"Oh that really isn't…" Jane began, then trailed off. "Necessary."

Maggie looped Jane's arm in hers, something Jane wasn't expecting to feel so calming. "We're so excited to have you with us. Those self-portraits we saw…" Maggie smiled in that way that only idols and grandmothers can. "Inspiring."

"Really?" Jane asked with a blush, walking with her to the door. "You liked them?"

"Oh honey, they were the best we've seen in a while. And if I may speak for the both of us…" Maggie stopped at the door, offering a glance backwards to her husband. "You're even more beautiful in person. You've got such great color."

With Jane still processing this string of compliments from otherworldly figures, Maggie opened the door for the trio, and they entered.

Jane, being a color-oriented person, first noticed the tone of the wallpaper, a blue-green almost something like Maggie's cardigan. A soothing, cool color, although Jane supposed that was the point; why would anyone choose to live in a house with agitating colors?

"Harold, why don't you put Jane's bags in her room while I give her a tour." Maggie suggested, leading Jane by the arm. "Over here is the dining room, although I can't remember the last time we dined in it. Now it's where we store the pieces we're about to sell."

And so it went, Maggie leading Jane through each room of the house, giving its technical name, a short quip, and its actual usage. Drawing room, Kitchen, Foyer, Great Hall, Pantry, Library, Study, Bedrooms, the like. Most were really used to store paint or canvas or paintings of some sort. All were furnished in cool tones, blues and greens, marked with the browns of oak armchairs and cabinets and bookshelves. So when her eyes caught a flash of red from the corner, Jane noticed.

"What's that?" She asked, pointing through the door where she had seen the bright hue.

Maggie smiled at the door. "That, Jane, is our most finicky project, Harold and I. Would you like to see it?" Without waiting for an answer, she started walking that way. Jane followed behind her, arm bent in an awkward tradition from the rapid change in direction.

The depth of the artwork hit her first. It felt as if she had wandered through a portal from a forest at dusk to the wide red plains of Hell.

For it was a landscape of hell, painted in the room: a panorama with such mastery of perspective and scale to rival the Sistine Chapel. In the center was a little stool, set over a tightly placed red dot, around which distorted figures twisted in some ill form.

Maggie gave Jane a look over. "You're about my height." She said. "It'll work. Go on, stand on the stool, please."

Jane laid a ginger foot on top of the stool before standing up, and the world changed.

In her later reflections on the topic, she described it to herself as the difference between watching a screen and going into virtual reality. All around her spread out scenes of torture, death, imprisonment and attempted escape, splashed with rivers and walls of fire.

And, despite not being at all like anything she expected from two mild-mannered minds like the Wallowfords, it was beautiful.

"How-" Jane tore her eyes away from the morbidity- "How did you mix these colors? The reds are so…"

"So red?" Maggie asked. "Yes, Harold and I are proud of the color. We don't mix it the same way each time. Makes the flames more real."

Jane nodded, eyes drawn away from Maggie to a tiny figure in the far background, her millimeter sized skin being flayed off with toothpick levels of detail. "Much more real."

Days passed at the Wallowford's rather regularly, which surprised Jane, considering the novelty of it all. Breakfast came out at 6:30 sharp, and despite waking up at a brisk six, she still managed to end up late due to losing her way briefly.

"You'll get used to it." Maggie reassured her. "I don't think we've had a single student not get lost a few times, have we Harold?"

"Last boy would get good'n lost." Harold chuckled through his toast. "Had to spend half a day trying to find him sometimes."

Maggie smiled. "Oh, poor kid. You should have met him, Jane. He could get lost in his own room if you let him."

Harold nodded. "His family said he'd always been like that."

Jane tensed at the table, but managed to relax and continue spooning scrambled eggs onto her plate without too much of a jerk.

Maggie turned in her chair. "How's your family?" She asked. "We never really get to learn about *who* the applicants are until they're here."

Jane, who had almost managed to get some of the eggs in her mouth before Maggie asked, put her hand down with a slow twirl of her fork, and put on her 'explaining' smile. "Don't really have any."

Typically, this is where older women would have given their best 'Bless your heart' sigh, the older men would frown and look at the floor, and someone would say, 'Oh, that's so awful'. Jane had given those exact lines every time someone asked about her family.

So when Harold burst out with an "Well that's lucky," and a chuckle, Jane barely kept her knee from hitting the table.

Harold shrugged. "It would make Isolationism easier for you, if you wanted."

"Excuse me?" Jane bought herself some time to process.

"Harold." Maggie complained. "I told you not to bring up the future so quickly."

"But I can't wait." Harold said. "You know how excited I get when they make the plunge."

"What?" Jane asked. "What plunge?"

"I'm sorry." Maggie spared an annoyed look up at her husband before continuing. "My husband likes to speak in metaphors. He means when," She gave another pointed look at Harold. "*If*, you decide to become like us and our other students."

"You mean, like," Jane paused. "Live in a house on my own and just do art? Never see anyone ever again?"

"Not necessarily." Harold butted in. "Our first, Talia, told us she's started to take students, like we do."

Maggie looked up at her husband, paused, then looked back at Jane. "But for the most part, no. You don't see anyone. At all. Even for the amazing benefits it provides for your art, it's not a decision to be taken lightly, or even considered so early in the program." She finished the sentence with increasing volume while shifting her gaze to her husband.

Harold, by this point, had made himself comfortable in his chair and had on what could only be described as an adoring smile. "I'm sorry, Maggie."

They laughed together, like something about the way he said it was some sort of inside joke. "As am I… always so cranky in the morning." And nothing more was said, bar a request for butter from across the table and a brief discussion of typical schedule.

By the week's end Jane had completely rethought her whole conception of art on three separate occasions. The Wallowfords encouraged her to doodle at every time imaginable. In little strategically placed bins, they kept spare notepads and sharpened pencils: by corners, windows, doorways, even bathrooms. As a woman cursed by the same pea-sized bladder of her father, the notebooks in the bathroom nearest her bedroom quickly filled with her attempts at drawing the far eye in ¾ view.

She quickly grew into a routine. She would wake up for breakfast, where the Wallowfords would be in their complementary-colored cardigans, and after, she would walk with Maggie in their backyard. Their conversations about art theory in their garden astounded her. One could imagine her a fledgling Plato in the presence of Socrates, gaining floral inspiration for her future Lyceum.

"Art, ultimately, isn't something we really control." Maggie said one upset, misty morning.

Jane shook her head and frowned. "What do you mean?" She asked. "We choose what we make, right? Someone's gotta choose to do it." Someone has to be there to do it.

In spite of herself, she thought of her mother, the embodiment of the executive decision. From having kids to moving away with her to even applying to the program in the first place: choices everywhere, and she made them all.

"Yes, of course, that's all true," She opened her eyes towards Jane. "But all the little pieces? Why a streak of red there, as opposed to over there? Why a leaflet in precisely that position as opposed to any other?" She shook her head. "No, we think we control Art, but in our subconscious, it's Art that rules, not any human rationale."

Jane sat back to chew on that thought for a while.

"Not that it's really all a big deal." Maggie chuckled, waving away a bug. "We just let our colors come out, don't we?" She smiled at Jane. "And you, as I have said, have got such great color."

Pondering thoughts like that, she would wander her way through the house, picking objects at random to still-life, until it was time for lunch. She always told herself she chose at random, but no matter what, she always ended up gravitating towards the Red Room. She didn't feel comfortable inside, not without either Maggie or Harold present, but she'd end up in the room adjacent, cutting glances from a vase to her notebook to the Room and back again. It was the color-contrast, she told herself, the brown and green of the rest of the Manor and the deep red of the Room, that made her keep going there. And if it wasn't, she supposed, it was just further proof that Art ruled the subconscious.

After lunch she would join the couple in the dining room, where they did most of their painting. At least, Maggie looked like she was painting. Harold had scrunched himself behind a microscope, working with what looked like a steampunk toothpick.

"You wanna look?" He asked, extricating himself when he saw her staring. "Here, let me zoom out."

The image that greeted Jane when she looked through the eyepiece was far from what she expected. She had to check what was on the slide and then what she saw again a few times just to make sure it was real.

Harold smiled, hefting the steampunk toothpick the way soldiers lovingly heft their weapons in bloody movies. "Had it made specially for me. It can paint lines down to the micrometer."

Jane stepped back. "That's… That's…"

"New York City." He finished. "On a postage stamp."

"There are people in the windows." Jane objected. "That's insane."

"More than you know." Harold laughed aloud, maneuvering himself back into position. "What is art anyway, but brief insanity?"

Jane found she didn't quite have an answer for that, so she returned to her work.

By the end of the next week Jane knew that she could not return to the normal world with all of its tedious tasks after having spent what already felt like an age in paradise, and said as much at the dinner table.

Harold and Maggie exchanged a look across the table, then smiled.

"That's fantastic." Harold said.

"I'm so proud." Maggie nodded. "I know it's never an easy decision to... abandon humanity."

"Yeah, um, about that," Jane put down her fork and managed to swallow her mashed potatoes. "Do you guys mind if I call someone?" She asked. Somewhere she remembered it was rude to leave a party without at least talking to the host, so she was sure it was rude to choose to live alone for the rest of your life and not tell your family.

"Of course not." Maggie reassured her. "In fact I'd encourage it, and you can start Isolationism tomorrow."

"If you would, though…" Harold eyed the other room. "New voices are a little shocking to me, and I've only just gotten used to yours."

If only a little put off by how strange the phrasing was, Jane got up and left. "Yeah, of course."

Harold gazed at his wife. "It always amazes me how you do that. A whole year since you've heard a new voice and you act as though you had just met people last week."

Maggie smirked. "And a good thing too. Otherwise, we wouldn't have any students."

"Oh, I don't know." Harold said. "A free ticket to fabulous riches seems like plenty of incentive, right? Besides," He laughed. "With their skills, they can either be our students or do check fraud, really. Not much of a choice."

Maggie laughed. "As if check fraud could make as much money."

Jane made her way to the bathroom near her room, which for some reason seemed the most private place of the Manor. She took a breath, closed her eyes, and dialed a number from memory.

"Hello-" For a moment, she thought her brother had picked up- "You've reached Grant Fischer. I'm sorry I couldn't catch your call. Please leave your name, number, and message."

BEEP.

For a moment, she thought, but decided to hang up. What message do you leave when you've been gone so long? She shook her head, glancing to a Face she had drawn the night before, peering out at her from the bin.

"No point." She told her Face. She'd have warned him about the upcoming small bladder problems he'd inherit, but if he didn't already know it, his Dad would explain it.

Her Face didn't respond.

She turned on her phone again, then put it back down. No one else to call. Her mom had been the one encouraging her to apply in the first place. Besides, she had always wanted Jane to act more like her, and if making decisions without consulting anyone resembled anyone, it resembled Mom.

She shrugged, half-smile towards her Face. "Might as well go for it."

When she came back to the table, the Wallowfords had just finished laughing about something. Not even laughing; to Jane it almost looked like Maggie was giggling. They brought their faces under control and turned to her.

"Jane," Maggie said. "We have a little…" She glanced at Harold and then back again. "Celebration, for this momentous decision in your art, and in your life. Would you like to see?" Neither Harold nor Maggie could contain their smiles that had surely not five seconds ago had been laughter, and Maggie always had an infectious smile.

Jane found herself smiling too. If she was going to be a recluse the rest of her life, she might as well enjoy a little party. "Yeah, sure." She said. "Lead the way."

So their little train processed, Maggie then Jane then Harold.

Jane realized where they were going, but didn't say anything. She liked the suspense.

The contrast, as it always did, hit Jane first. Everywhere, from the wallpaper to the furniture to Maggie's cardigan to Harold's pants were soft, brown and green and earthy. So even the briefest angled glimpse of the interior of the Red Room dragged the eye towards it. Inside, Jane could see the whacked-out mini paintbrush Harold had been using on the floor.

"So," She shrugged, trying not to look so closely at any of the torture scenes around her. It was hard. "What's up?"

Maggie smiled. "How do you like it?"

Jane shook her head, eyes wide. "Like everything you two touch… incredible."

"How would you like to be part of it?" Maggie asked.

Jane looked around at the walls now, looking at the faces wrenched in pain. "What, like a model? Are all your students here?"

"Not the way you're thinking." Harold said, jamming his mini paintbrush into the flesh underneath the point of Jane's chin.

"God!" He swore. "I hated that damned stamp." He ripped out the bulky toothpick. Blood burst Jane's neck like a water gun. Harold caught her before she fell, guiding her head with an artist's hand, each spurt of her blood making a new wall of flame. "And that God-forsaken microscope."

Maggie ran around the corner and came back with the other painting supplies. Together they worked through the night, adding a new scene to their hellscape and chuckling at how easy this year had been. No family to deal with, and her art was so easy to imitate, unlike their last student. Harold griped on quite a bit further about him, his tool, his stamps, and his microscopic style.

"She's got such great color." Maggie appreciated, stepping over Jane to view her progress further from the wall.

Harold nodded. "She really does, doesn't she?" His face broke out into a vision of pride. "Our masterpiece."

"Our masterpiece." Maggie paused and leaned to give her husband a kiss on the cheek, then spread a little more of Jane's Color on the wall.

No, I got it wrong in the beginning. Everyone knows *of* the Wallowfords.

Strings Attached

Everyone knows about Orr Enterprises. The OE logo sat on everything; trucks, ships, railroads, boxes. Anything that moved or got moved. Not to mention on the uniforms of what seemed like a third of the population.

More importantly to Kelly, the OE laid upon one mail truck that carried a letter (also graced with the OE logo) she had been waiting on for some time. She had to use her power five times a day this week just to keep calm.

Now that it was here, on her lap, in her room, she didn't know what to do with herself. The tips of her fingers tingled across the edges of the paper until she found a place in the flap she could use to open it.

She opened it. Read it. Read it again, this time tensing a little on her String so she could focus properly. The paper flittered to the floor as she began a little happy dance. One line ran through her head over and over. Show up in a Grey OE Uniform Blazer and Slacks.

Kelly was now a member of Orr Enterprises.

The face of an empire, Maximilian Orr smiled, the flashing of cameras no longer causing him to squint like they used to do.

"Mister Orr, Mister Orr!" Reporters called. "What are your plans with your infrastructure?"

"Have you heard about the situation in the Congo?"

"What was your inspiration?"

Orr stopped at that one. He had responses for them all, of course, very precise ones at that, but he was stressed, and for once he wanted to be able to answer an easy question.

"My inspiration?" He asked into the microphone. The crowd hushed, the chosen reporter stepping close with a recorder. "I wasn't old enough to remember the Culls, the Powerism, or those other things our Citizens with Powers were put through."

The crowd stood stock-still. Nothing like bringing up atrocity to get people's attention.

"I did, however, remember going to the newly integrated elementary schools, and, frankly, feeling a little bit jealous. Understandably, I think. Nothing wrong with wanting to be special."

Orr spread his arms wide, pulling his sleeves down to expose his forearms. He couldn't help it. He looked down at his shadow. It stood still, like he did, but he still couldn't help but imagine it winking back at him.

"Look." He said anyway, gesturing to his forearms, free of the thin line all Powerful people had there. "I'm a plain old man. But I wanted to be a beacon of hope, and a message, that with or without Powers, everyone can do great things."

The reporters nodded, some clapped, some even cheered. Orr turned away and let his Public Aide tell everyone he'd be taking no more questions tonight.

Kelly struggled to keep up with Martha, who was almost more uptight than her graying bun and the precise clacking of her three-inch heels on the marble floor.

"You will bring him his coffee every morning at six-thirty precisely, and his dinner every night at nine." She informed her. "He doesn't eat lunch. You will take his laundry here," She pointed to the chute to her right. "And pick it up down there." She pointed to the stairs on her left. "In between your duties, you will be available at any time for him to contact you." She stopped and whirled around, poking a pin into the lapel of Kelly's blazer and drawing blood behind it in her carelessness. "When this buzzes, you will report to his quarters with all haste."

Kelly shut her eyes to force herself not to roll them. *All haste.* She imitated in her mind.

She pulled on her String. If she was going to have to work under that lady, she might as well get used to it and not be riled up all the time.

"What, sleeping on the job already?" Martha called, already halfway down the hall. "Please keep up."

Kelly shook her head, following her. *Please keep up.*

Orr closed his door behind him, letting his neck stretch in a double crackling pop. He locked the door, put his keys on one hook and his jacket on another.

Then for the harder part. He walked his fingers through his hair, looking for it and searching until he found his String and tugged.

String was more of a misnomer for him. For people with Powers, apparently, it really felt like a string, like those of a puppet: pull gently and watch the world dance. For him, it was more like the release cord on a parachute, yanked on with all his might to accomplish the same thing every time.

He shuddered at the crawling sensation he still hadn't gotten used to, even after all these years. It felt like a cape coming off his back, but far more slowly than the way gravity would have done it. He supposed it would feel more natural to someone who didn't have their String forced on them.

Orr flipped on the light, and in front of him laid his Shadow. It waved, then glided across the floor to the two computers on the bench, overlooking the city many stories below. It sat and began typing.

"Hello to you too."

The only break his Shadow took from clacking away was to lift one hand to wave him over.

"Fine, fine." Orr walked over to the other computer. "It's not as though we can destroy the world tomorrow."

As he sat down, he could have sworn his Shadow laughed.

The buzzing of her pin on her nightstand woke Kelly sharper than any alarm clock she had ever owned. She blinked, rubbing her eyes until they decided to focus. What time was it anyway. Five? He really needed her at five in the morning?

Groaning, she got up, throwing on her uniform. It was wrinkly, but if Orr wanted her to look professional, he should've called for her at a reasonable hour.

Orr had to hand it to himself. His company really did control everything.

With a few clicks on a keyboard, the Trans-Siberian Railroad collapsed. Now half of Russia wouldn't be able to get any food.

With another few, he breached the safety measures at the OE-CDC, releasing a whole host of plagues across south-eastern America.

There had at one point been a shipment of medicine sailing for the malaria-stricken Democratic Republic of the Congo. At one point.

Electrical grid, gone. Radio towers, gone. Postal service, gone.

So he and his Shadow went, going one by one and ensuring the deaths of thousands, millions, billions. Catastrophe on a worldwide scale. He held the strings of infrastructure that controlled the world. Now, with his tugging and pulling, he watched it dance to its own funeral dirge.

Orr wondered if somewhere, out there, the man who gave him his String all those years ago was laughing.

Kelly knocked on the door and had to jump out of the way because Orr answered it so quickly. She bit down a curse.

"Hello, Mister Orr. You called for me… Are you okay?"

Orr rubbed the shadows under his eyes. "No. Come in."

Kelly followed him into the modern suite. Across the room, two closed laptops sat on a pretty fantastic looking desk, facing a massive window.

"Um…" She began. "Why did you ask for me?"

He sat down on a sleek black couch. "I understand you have a Power, something to do with the human body."

She nodded. "I can slow your heartbeat, close off your adrenal glands. Basically make you calm down. Put you to sleep."

Orr bent over, putting his head between his knees. "If you don't mind, I'm rather in need of that at the moment."

"Of- of course." She said. She pulled.

Kelly didn't realize Orr wasn't casting a shadow until the sun's rays peeked through the window behind him.

Mama D

Everyone knows Mama D. She runs the little apothecary on Sycamore Road. In the front window, there's a handwritten sign that says "Absolutely No Love Potions For Any Price". Below it, Mama D had tacked on an addition that read "Stop Asking".

Sal was late, and lost, which is always a perilous combination. He had just left the interstate for a burger and a leak, but he must have turned the wrong way out of the McDonalds, because this sure as hell wasn't the interstate. They were going to tear him apart at the sales meeting.

He pulled his red Talladega into a parking spot by the sidewalk under the shade of one of those pygmy trees that are planted in sidewalks to make towns look more quaint. He stretched out for the glove compartment in the hopes that he had left a map in there sometime before. He hadn't.

With a groan, he looked around for somewhere where he might ask for directions. With fortune (whether good or ill I'll leave for you to decide) just on the other side of the pygmy tree he caught sight of Mama D's famous sign.

"Love potions." He snorted. It was probably run by a quack, but said quack was also probably an old lady who knew the area well. They typically were. He might have to waste a few dollars on a bottle of colored water, but he could be out of there and on his way in a few minutes if he played his cards right. Plan in mind and keys in hand, he wriggled himself out of the too-small car door and waddled into the Apothecary.

A bell above the door frame tinkled with excitement at a new customer. "I'll be right with you," an old voice croned. An old lady who probably knew the area well, just as he suspected. "Look at anything you want, but don't touch. You're just as likely to grow three inches as turn into a frog."

Sal covered a snort. As a salesman himself, he had to admit a begrudging approval of her line. It might have helped ensnare someone less intelligent as he.

He maneuvered his paunch around the haphazard shelves filled with all sorts of glass bottles filled with what was surely just water and food coloring, reading labels to himself. Tincture of Henbane and Rosemary. Newt's Eye and New Moon Mint. What a sham.

"I'm Mama D." Sal nearly jumped as the old lady seemed to appear behind him. "How can I help you, honey?"

Sal recovered. "Hello ma'am." He had to tilt his head down to look her in the eye. How tall could she be, four-five? And older than dirt too. "I seem to be lost. Do you-"

"Yes, yes you are." Mama D interrupted him. "I have just the thing." With that, she disappeared behind another row of shelves.

"Um, ma'am," Sal tried to keep up with her without knocking over anything. He was reminded of the saying 'a Bull in a China Shop'. In this case, a fat man in an apothecary. "I really just need directions to the interstate."

"And a whole lot more." Her voice came from a completely different corner than he had expected. Advantages of being small and knowing where you were going, he supposed. "Over here, honey."

Sal worked himself around the corner of another shelf to see Mama D, standing beside what looked like a copper sink. "Come." She said. "Put your hands into the basin."

He put his hands up by his ears and repeated his line. "I really just need directions to the interstate."

Mama D didn't so much respond as merely tilt her head to the side and raise an elderly eyebrow in an unmistakable message. If you ever want to find the interstate, you'll put your hands in the stupid sink and humor an old woman. Sal heard it loud and clear. He let go, rolled up his sleeves, and zoned out while the old lady did her thing.

Her thing was more in depth than he had anticipated, full of murmured chants and the addition of so many different colored waters and other ingredients that Sal lost count. His hands were now fully submerged, and he could have sworn he felt something touch him, although Mama D was careful not to touch the frothy mix that now reached halfway up his forearms.

"You've got such a beautiful shop." Sal found himself saying, although he wasn't sure why.

Mama D didn't look up from her work. "Thanks, honey."

Sal resolved to tell everyone at the sales meeting about this little place. Once he got there. He felt the potion bubbling at his elbows.

Mama D snapped, and Sal's eyes shut.

Sal accelerated on the merging ramp to the interstate. In the cupholder he had some ginseng and wormwood in ether for confidence in his sales meeting, a few other vials in his glove compartment for later, and in his jacket pocket he had twenty of Mama D's business cards.

It should be said that Mama D never had problems making ends meet.

Folie a Deux

Everyone knows you don't fuck with Witches.

Sean slipped off his soaked saddle and tied his horse to the post by the lights of the Tavern, fumbling with the wet reins and his gloved hands. Happy Birthday to him, he grumbled. As a treat, he could sit in the rain for hours, drink whiskey better suited to stripping paint than enjoying, and (maybe) sleep in a cot without bed bugs.

In the dark, Sean nearly tripped over a stack of a few pitchforks leaning by the door. He smirked. Farmers. What can you do?

Inside was dry, tolerably warm, and better yet, empty but for a huddle of locals muttering over a table in the corner. They all had typical black-grey Heklion hair, he noted, although that's not too much of a surprise out this far from anything. He supposed they owned the pitchforks.

Sean flicked back his hood, finally realizing how badly his back had bowed in his latest escape - *change of scenery*, as he preferred to call them. As he cracked his back, his gloves came off too, and he got the chance to blow some much-needed warm air into his frozen joints.

He caught the bartender's eye as he sat down. "Drink and a room." He too, was a Heklion, wearing one of their religious images around his neck.

The tender rummaged around in his pocket and retrieved a key. "Room..." He checked the tag as he put it down. "Four. And to drink?"

"Whiskey." Sean said, reaching into his own pocket for his cigarettes and matchbook.

The bartender shook his head. "Can't smoke in here."

Sean frowned, looking around here. He could've sworn he smelled tobacco smoke in here, and he was right. "He's smoking." He pointed into the far corner, where an old man he hadn't seen earlier sat on a stool, blowing smoke rings through each other.

"He's different." The tender insisted. "He's Gerd, and he's smoking a pipe. Completely different."

Sean sighed, bit down a few choice remarks about the brains of these Heklion hicks, and gathered himself. "What's your name?"

The bartender frowned. "Drake."

"Alright then." Sean said. "Drake?"

"Uh-huh?" said Drake.

"I can't very well smoke out there." Sean pointed to the door, where outside it still rained, and heavier than before. "And there is no difference, smell or otherwise, between smoking a pipe and smoking a cigarette." And he'd be damned before he'd let anyone keep him from smoking on his birthday.

The older man in the corner laughed. "Let the poor fool smoke, Drake." He spat out another ring, which settled over his head like a halo. "Just finding his own death faster anyhow."

Sean breathed in deep, pulled out a cigarette, and pointed it at the man. "I'm no fool." He said to no one in particular, lighting up.

The old man just smiled.

Drake placed the whiskey on the bar. "Three Copper." He said. "And a Silver for the room."

Sean gave up the cash, grumbling. Drake was overcharging, and Sean was running low on funds. Having a lot of daring escapes and changes of scenery is cool and sexy, but it's also a symptom of being a poor thief, without money, loot, or skill.

"You're leaving!" The group in the other corner broke up, with all but one heading for the door, to the one's dismay. "What about your pride? What about Victor?"

"Victor's deader than a doornail, Cara." One of the leaving group replied. "And that's exactly how you'll be if you don't give this up."

"He wasn't afraid to die." said Cara.

From somewhere in the depths of the group, someone said, "He didn't have time to be afraid, he was dead so damn fast."

This was, evidently, not the thing to say, as Cara got in a decisive three steps forward while pulling something sharp from her pocket before the first speaker and another person intercepted her, arm in arm, and began pulling her away.

Sean chuckled, now engrossed in the little drama put before him as birthday entertainment. "Go for the nuts, Cara!" He cheered under his breath.

She neither heard nor took Sean's advice, which is a good rule of thumb. Instead, Cara got placed in a chair and admonished, "Leave Alassiel alone," by the original speaker, who now, placed side by side with Cara, looked similar enough to be siblings.

"You're a coward, Fabian." She spat. "You're as yellow as the piss in your breeches when you think of that *zheti* Witch and her staff."

This caught Sean's attention. He was, after all, a thief by trade, and while murderous witches in the wilderness aren't good news, he knew quite a few people who would pay well for a bonafide magical item. They don't typically just fall into your lap like that one did, almost like an evening birthday present.

"Victor's already dead." Fabian said, without turning or stopping. "The only thing you'll find looking for vengeance is your own death." He closed the door behind him, and they were alone: Cara, Sean, the old man, and Drake.

Silence reigned, and no one stood challenger for what seemed like quite some time.

Sean figured if no one else was going to speak, he might as well begin working on Cara- *introducing himself*, as he preferred to call it. "I know it's not my place to ask," He began, receding into what he called his *stage persona*. "But as a concerned stranger, who was Victor?"

"He's a cousin." Cara said, her Heklion accent so thick that it sounded to Sean like 'Eeza coozin'. "And blood to half the men there who just walked away, even though that puss filled *zheti* Witch still breathes and lives and wastes the air."

That word again, *zheti*. Sean figured it was some Heklion oath and left it at that. He pursed his lips, nodding. "I'm so sorry for your loss."

"I don't need your *Filkithi* pity!" From the way she spat Sean sensed she had called his pity something much worse than the Witch. "Either help me kill her or leave me be, stranger."

He shrugged. She was too the point, but he supposed that would make nicking the staff easier. "My name's Sean." He sat down, lighting his next cigarette with the end of his last. "Now where would this djeti Witch be hiding?"

Cara smirked. "*Zheti*." She corrected. "And let me draw you a map."

The next morning, he didn't need it. There was something approximating a path from the outskirts of the village through the woods, from so many townsfolk seeking cures or, in this case, violence. Just before Sean walked over the ridge of the hill before him, Cara grabbed his shoulder and pulled him behind an outcropping of rock. "Her hut's just over the rise." She hissed. "Remember the plan?"

"We didn't make a plan!" Sean hissed back.

"Fuckin' right." Cara said, drawing a long dirk from her boot. "Let's gut that *zheti* Witch."

With that, she charged over the hill, screaming.

After half of a second of shock, Sean rolled his eyes, jogging for the side window. Let the crazy Heklion hick distract the Witch long enough for him to nab her staff.

He heard more shouts, and something that sounded like whips, cracking one after the other. He felt that chill in his bones, straight from a fearful memory so old it had ossified into every human's very being. Magic. Shuddering past it, he pried open the window and rolled in.

Cara stood, knife in hand, by the doorway. Between them stood the Witch, from behind at least a rather unremarkable woman, if it weren't for the balls of fire that floated above each of her outstretched hands.

"You gonna help me or what?" Cara yelled.

Sean dove behind a chair as the Witch obliterated the section of floor where he had been. That's when he saw it. By the doorway, which Cara was unknowingly protecting from the Witch. The staff.

It was a small thing, maybe a yard long, made of wood, wrapped with cloth ribbons and topped with a pendant made of what looked like bits of a broken bottle.

Sean didn't so much make the decision to run than follow his well ingrained habit of acting solely for the benefit of his person. Staffs are magic, and therefore worth money. He had met Cara the day prior, and didn't much like her either. And Witches, as a general rule, are very dangerous. He wasn't going to let his birthday bonus get away from him. He felt like he made the right decision.

Cara cursed Sean while he ran, staff in hand. Moments later the Witch killed her where she stood.

One of the few benefits of being a failed thief is that you can run very fast. Sean, as it happened, prided himself on his ability to run. Somehow, even with his head start, he soon sensed rather than felt the Witch at his heels. That chill in his bones he thought he had shuddered away came back and in greater measure. That memory of Magic.

Something obstructed his stride as he felt her reach and miss for the staff. He tried to bend away from her, but she was still faster. The Witch, from the front just as unremarkable except that she was absolutely terrifying, redoubled her efforts and soon got a finger through the loop of the pendant.

"Aeletay." She shouted, obviously some magical keyword, and the ribbons sprung to life, unwrapping, expanding, and rewrapping, entangling all four arms involved. Her hands grasped the staff by the head almost like someone might pray, pendant and glass sticking out above each thumb. His hands held the staff more like one might hold one of the pitchforks he had seen last night at the Tavern. With a toothy grin, the Witch jumped up and delivered a double-legged kick to Sean. The blast of magic she added to the strike launched them yards from each other.

Sean gasped into the torn ribbons over his mouth, clutching his stomach with one hand but in the other…

Impossibly, he still had the staff. The pendant had broken off, and the ribbons had snapped nasty matching bruises across the fleshy bits between both of his thumbs and index fingers, but he still had it. He scrambled to his feet.

The Witch had already stood, hands outstretched, glass pendant in her right. Before Sean could feel that chill in his bones again, he put a hand on each end of the staff and braced it against his knee.

"I'll break it." He warned. "I will."

The Witch tilted her head, something nearly like a smile on her face. "You know, that girl in there cursed you to die. And something tells me her oath was heard."

"Not one step closer!"

"But why? We're bonded, you know." She raised her hands, displaying matching cuts on each hand where the glass had cut her skin. Exactly in the same place as his bruises. "Marked. Fool Thief and Failed Victim, Prisoner and Executioner."

"Shut up." Sean yelled. "I have the staff!" Just to prove it, he brandished it a bit.

The Witch rolled her eyes, tired of the game. With a flick of her wrist, she swung the bits of broken glass, slapping the staff out of Sean's hands and into a tree, snapping it in two.

She smirked. "That was a stick."

"Please!" He cried. "Please, it's my birthday."

The Witch grinned, lifting the glass shards above her head. "Then here's your birthday present."

Whether Sean died first because of that ancient chill in his bones, a heart attack, or the fireball, you might say he had a bad birthday indeed.

Andrej the Mime

Everyone knows about Andrej the Mime. They say he's the best mime in Paris, and that he never breaks character. The truth is so much worse.

Andrej lives in a clear box. Not just as part of his job, but his whole life. He eats by throwing baguettes over the top, and drinks his Parisian wine via waterfall.

He also doesn't talk to anyone. He doesn't try anymore, although he used to. When he did no one would hear him, so he doesn't try anymore. The same goes for all kinds of human contact, from shaking hands to high-fives and hugs.

There is no lock on his clear box, but there also isn't any key.

He sleeps in his box, although not well. It's hard to sleep with a shoulder stuck in the corner, and the blankets never warm him up enough.

He doesn't go out in the rain. The last time he did, the water pooled up to his knees before he could get inside and drain out again. He didn't need any nightmares to imagine what might have happened if he stayed. He got them anyway.

Sometimes, Andrej feels like his box is filling up again, like it did that day in the rain. These times he forgets his rules. He screams in his box, hoping someone would see him. He raises his hand for high-fives and makes a cardboard sign saying "Free Hugs", but no one obliges. He beats against the inside of his box for dear life, as if he had ever once seen it so much as buckle in his life, all in hopes that somehow, someway, he won't drown in his clear box.

He tries to climb out; he tries to lift up the bottom. He even once purchased a blowtorch. He's been to doctors and specialists, engineers and psychologists. He isn't sure who to believe anymore.

Yes, Andrej is confused, and more importantly, stuck. But most of all, he really, really, wants to be free.

So be kind to poor Andrej, if you see him on the street, give him a coin or a smile or a wave, lest you be cursed by his malady, and find yourself an entertainer to all, trapped in your own clear cage.

The Tale of Blanceor

I'll be honest with you here. Even I didn't know about this.

Franklin had drool dripping off his tusks in anticipation of his first Meal. Gerald, his Food-father, was beside him, creeping from the shadows of the bedroom closet, fur leaving an indistinct silhouette against the dim wall. He could feel his horns heating up in expectation. The prey was so close.

The huddled form of the child lay sleeping, curled beneath a Blanket, stuffed animal clutched in her arms. Franklin was so close he could see her eyeballs flitting about beneath her eyelids. She must have been in a *Grazt*, a dream. Claws extended, he reached for the child's leg, trembling in anticipation of his fangs ripping through her calf and finally fulfilling the *Furga* that had been driving his every action since he began to grow.

"Franklin!" Gerald hissed in their monstrous language. "What do you think you're doing?"

Franklin almost howled in frustration, which he would have done if he hadn't known it would wake the prey. "I hunger!"

"We must respect the Blanket." Gerald chided the younger *Montragt*. "She is Covered. We must leave."

"They don't even remember Blanceor anymore." Franklin whined. "I've been an Follower for six summers. I want to feed."

"They all know to Cover themselves." Countered Gerald, ignoring Franklin's complaint about his hunger. "If you really feel that the memory of Blanceor is slighted, why don't you remind the child?"

An exasperated sigh, a raised eyebrow in return. Resigned to his fate, Franklin stepped beside the girl's head and began to hum the deep sonitory tones of *Graztakt*: Dream-Speak.

"Once, in a time you've never known, in a land you won't remember, you Humans and we *Monstragti* lived at war…"

In her slumber, the girl was ripped from her vision of unicorns and her beloved bear Gabbie to a Stone-Age village, bustling with life. Baskets, full of fish and other goods, carried overhead by tanned women laboring in the sun bobbed and floated through the crowd from thatched hut to thatched hut. Children ran underneath the feet of the people, chasing each other and knocking over things in their hectic game.

But all was not at ease. Men stood alert along the log parapet, vicious spears at their side, eyes intently scanning the woods beyond for something - anything - that might signal danger. Other guards stood beside every hut, backs in the admirable posture of attention, wide bronze swords at their hips. Everyone, bar the oblivious playing children, had a look of fear in their eye, fear born of hard knowledge and harder experience. If the eyes are the windows to the soul, the observant bystander could get the sort of sneak peak that would cause most modern people to look away.

"MONSTERS!"

A frantic bell rang out, piercing the amiable quietness that had pervaded the village henceforth, and fear even seeped through the windows of the children, whose game paused the instant the first peal slammed into their ears. The parapet men scrambled along the walkway, carefully brandishing their spears, while the women dropped their ever-important baskets and fled to the nearest hut, children clutched in their arms. The guards by those huts ushered the civilians in, whispering comforting lies that didn't reach their eyes. Their eyes told the truth.

CRASH at the Gate, CRASH CRASH CRASH of brute furry bodies ramming their horns against the feeble wood that separated their *Furgai* from satiation, satiation in flesh and blood under their claws, muscle and bone between their fangs. Some of the Horde were so lost in their hunger that their horns left scorch marks in the Gate, such was their heat.

Arrows flew this way and that, father was ripped from family, and Follower was suddenly left Food-Fatherless. Howls and screams of pain and loss intermixed in the air even before the two sides met in earnest, one driven by hunger, the other by survival. All the while, the women and children and other sensible people hid.

With one final booming CRASH, the Gate fell, and the monstrous Followers, driven now by their *Furgai* and by revenge ripped through the cloud of dust that had been thrown up, goring the weak humans with their tusks as the slower Food-Fathers followed in on their hooves. Here the screams and howls reached a new pitch, and the women and children trembled in fear and tears in their hiding places.

Into this bloody melee came Blanceor.

"Dradrakaton mjeo Furga!" He screamed in the feral language his mouth was never meant to utter. *"Gde tat Ugtert sigula?"*

Feed the Food-Father of all Food-Fathers to me! Where does that Follower hide?

Monstragti looked up from their vicious meal to gawk at this Human that dared Dream-Speak, that had the audacity to challenge their Overlord. In another guttural shout, he repeated his challenge, brandishing his sole armament in the air: a square of cloth.

Silence was the only answer given to Blanceor, bar the groans of those meals who hadn't yet perished. Bloody maws gaped at this incursion into their feeding, tusks still dripping in drool and gore.

"Sratati!" He spat.

Children!

His eyes rolled back to gaze at the mind within, and he dropped into a *Dayizgrazt*, a daydream, to find the Food-Father of all Food-Fathers who refused to answer his challenge. His whole face twitched and convulsed for agonizing minutes; no Human was made for Dream-Magic, but no *Monstragt* dared interrupt a *Dayizgrazt*, no matter who was performing it. Somehow, before Blanceor collapsed in a heap of exhaustion and eternal sleep, he broke into a triumphant "Ha!" and awoke.

"I've found you!" He called in his native English. "Come and fight me, you coward!"

In the huts whispers flitted this way and that between mother and child.

Blanceor. Blanceor. Blanceor will save us.

And then, lumbering between the two shredded logs that had once been the edges of the Gate, came Izgnat, *Dradrakat* of all *Monstragti*.

Lumbering he came, not walking. Lumbering was the only word fit for the frame of Izgnat, which towered twice as high as any *Monstragt*, the shortest of whom was already head and shoulders above Blanceor, who was large for a human. His horns, normally only the size of a human finger, swept wide enough that they could fit around the huts in which the women and children cowered, his fangs were the size of Blanceor's hands, tusks long enough to puncture three or four men cleanly. His nostrils flared wide, smell of fresh meat overpowered by the cloyingly sweet stench of a *Dayigrazt*. His rippling arms reached nearly down to his knees; claws were the only weapon he carried, claws and the brute strength that made him the Food-Father of all Food-Fathers. His fur was matted and bloody, his hooves chipped.

Blanceor not one step backwards took.

A pang of *Furga* came over Izgnat, for not even the mighty are free of that ever-seeking hunger, and without a second thought he stoperred it with the nearest breathing body to his arm: in this case, a dying Human soldier who barely had time to scream before he was swallowed whole.

Having been fed, Izgnat let out a bellow that shook the very earth beneath him, lowered his massive tusks and charged. Stably stood Blanceor, holding out his cloth as if by sheer force of will it would halt the inexorable charge of Izgnat. *Monstragti* howled in laughter as they saw what they thought would certainly be the death of this strange human. The tips of Izgnat's tusks lowered to the level of Blanceor's stomach, horns sizzling the air in anticipation of ripping through his spine. He took the final lumbering step.

But Blanceor's spine was not there.

Izgnat's hot right horn left a long scorch mark along Blanceor's cloth as they passed each other by, but Blanceor remained unscathed, standing just to the left of where he had been.

Monstragti howled once more, this time in frustration as the human was not yet dead. Izgnat whirled around, fury enflamed by this puny being even more than it had been before. Again he charged, horns so hot they created their own mirage around them. Again Blanceor was not there when the charge came. Again the charge, tips of Izgnat's horns catching fire with so much heat. Again, no satiation, no death.

Izgnat whirled around once more, this time determined to slaughter the Human wherever it stood. Nearby logs burst into flame as his horns passed them by; only to be snuffed out by the wind caused by his passing. Blanceor stood stolidly. Surely this would be the end of Blanceor, Swift of Foot. He jumped neither left nor right.

He jumped up.

The Cloth of Blanceor he trailed behind him as he did so, and Izgnat's face became entrapped by the leather. Snorting and coughing, he tried to dislodge it, but the more Izgnat struggled the more it became entangled in his fangs and tusks and fur. Slowly suffocating in its embrace, he tried to scratch it off with his claws, but the cloth held firm, seemingly a being of its own, forcing its way down Izgnat's mouth and nose.

He lumbered this way, then that way, then finally collapsed with a THUD that knocked down nearby trees.

Atop the fallen one Blanceor stood, retrieving his Cloth, and looked every *Monstragti* in the eyes.

"*Gasta tjet Blanceton!*"

Remember you the Blanket!

"So Cover yourself, little human." Franklin finished. "For all *Monstragti* must remember, even when you forget."

"Come now, Gerald." The Food-Father put a protective arm around his Follower, leading him away from the child's bedside. "Let us find an Uncovered one for you to feed upon."

The Maniac King

Everyone knows the Maniac King on the Bakery step. He was long in the tooth but his beard is longer, and his stare is the longest of them all. He mumbles and shambles and doesn't speak. The Baker lets him eat bread scraps for free, even though he scares small children and dogs. He was supposedly a king, from the Ancient and Venerable Line of *Ggyldir*, but the only showers he took were the ones the gods blessed on the fields, and his rags were black with dirt.

The first meal Dan brought the *Ilver* was bread and an apple for breakfast, which meant he picked up a loaf from the Bakery. The Maniac King mumbled something as he passed, but Dan ignored him, like he had learned to do years ago, fetching bread for people less important than the *Ilver*.

The *Ilver* sat in the window frame above his door, as was his habit, and so Dan brought the meal there.

"*Ilver*." Dan called.

"Ah, yes." The man waved a pale gaunt arm, not turning his head. "Bring it here." He didn't turn to face Dan until the plate was practically in his lap. "Thank you." Then, naturally, he chose to make direct eye contact, with grey eyes that blended darker into his pupil, and hold it.

"Um, of course." Dan tried to nod, then decided to just walk away.

The *Ilver* looked back outside, then down at the bread, taking it in his hands and smelling it deeply. "Fresh baked bread. Did you see King Eliah the First on the way?"

Dan frowned. He barely even recognized the beggar by the door that morning. "Who?"

"King Eliah Daniel Hillitholn Ggyldrine the First!" The *Ilver* protested. "He would have been your ruler, sixty years ago. How short the memory of youth. Besides, you share one of his names. You ought to know his history."

That didn't clarify much for Dan, given that he was twelve and the oldest person he knew was forty-seven, but there was only one person he could mean. "You're telling me the Maniac King is over sixty years old?"

"Don't call him that." The *Ilver* said. "He's a victim of horrible atrocities, and he has Syllvyne Qong's Royal Blood in him."

"What happened?"

The *Ilver* smiled. "I believe there is a more formal way to ask an *Ilver* for a story."

Dan blushed and looked away. "My apologies, I spoke out of line."

"Forget it." He said. "I didn't write his story, the gods did, and the gods' stories are free to everyone." He pointed. "Sit. I'll tell you. Luckily for you, the gods write better stories than I do, sometimes."

Before Eliah was king, he had to win a succession war against his cousin. It was a quarrel that could have been solved with a little less inbreeding and a little less greed, but such are hard things to ask from nobility at times. The scrap got a bit desperate on both sides as they each lost more men and gold, until, at the final battle at Filleot, west of here, King Eliah killed his cousin and won with less than eighty men to spare. He ruled stably thereafter for two decades.

It came to be that a Black mage infested the Ggyldrine Tower nearby. King Eliah joined the Coalition of local Kings that arose to purge the mage, but he fell afoul of the Coalition Council, gathered his own army, and rode out to defeat the mage alone. The Black mage routed his army, capturing King Eliah and much of his retinue.

The Black mage could, on an individual basis, control minds. He had one of Eliah's own guards torture him for information about the Coalition he didn't have. That guard had been a fellow survivor of Filleot. After every beating, every cut, and every strike, King Eliah tried to break the mage's spell by reminding the guard of it.

Filleot, he would shout, then say, then whisper, then breathe. Filleot.

The mage realized within a day the king knew nothing, and emboldened by his earlier success, he decided to march out against the rest of the Coalition. After raiding our countryside for a year, he was finally defeated, the tower reclaimed, and King Eliah freed. By then, however, after so much torture from within and without, there was nothing to be done for the King's mind. He could do naught but eat, shit, and say Filleot.

He had no direct heirs, so the throne went to one of the cousin's sons, and has passed through since. Exactly how it would have been before Filleot. The new King had not forgotten his father's death at Eliah's lance that fateful day, and threw him onto the streets, despite his condition. Few lords had either the money or the disposition to help him, given the Black mage's yearlong pillage.

"So he wandered," The *Ilver* finished. "Until he found a bit of shade and a steady source of food, and has remained there since."

Dan bowed from his seat, then stood up and bowed again. "That was an excellent story, *Ilver*."

"If you say so, then it was."

Dan didn't really know what to make of that for an answer, but the *Ilver* seemed content to leave the conversation at that, and so did he. He left the *Ilver* looking out the window, and walked home.

The next day, Dan went on the same trip to fetch the *Ilver*'s morning apple and bread, and passed King Eliah.

He stared at Dan, then frowned. "Filleot." He hissed.

Dan shook his head. "Not me."

"Filleot." Eliah grunted. "Filleot."

Dan shuddered. "Yeah." He said, if only to get him to shut up. "Filleot."

Eliah smiled for the first time in a while. He had only three teeth left, each of them rimmed in green. Dan hurried away to tend to the *Ilver*. Had he looked long enough, he would have seen how the moss and decay on his teeth complimented the green in his eyes, which shone with a new light upon the simple recognition, the three syllables he had wanted to hear for so long.

www.ingramcontent.com/pod-product-compliance
Lightning Source LLC
Chambersburg PA
CBHW061447160726
47995CB00003B/1080